CAPTAIN CODSWALLOP
and the
FLYING KIPPER

MICHAEL COX

CAPTAIN CODSWALLOP
and the
FLYING KIPPER

Illustrated by Kelly Waldek

A & C Black • London

First published 2006 by
A & C Black Publishers Ltd
38 Soho Square, London, W1D 3HB

www.acblack.com

Text copyright © 2006 Michael Cox
Illustrations copyright © 2006 Kelly Waldek

The rights of Michael Cox and Kelly Waldek to be
identified as the author and illustrator of this work respectively
have been asserted by them in accordance with the
Copyrights, Designs and Patents Act 1988.

ISBN: 0-7136-7630-2
ISBN: 978-0-7136-7630-3

A CIP catalogue for this book is available from the British Library.

A & C Black uses paper produced with elemental chlorine-free
pulp, harvested from managed sustained forests.

Printed and bound in Great Britain by Bookmarque Ltd, Croydon

CHAPTER ONE

In the year of 1588, a battered, old pirate ship full of battered, old pirates was making its way up the River Thames towards Old London Town. The pirate ship was called the *Grumpy Roger*. It was painted bright green and covered with patches of all shapes and sizes that covered the dozens of holes in its creaking timbers. Flying from its main mast was an enormous and extremely tatty pair of underpants painted with a skull and crossbones.

A large, cheerful-looking man with a warty nose, missing teeth and big, gold earrings was standing on the bridge. He was dressed in a velvet waistcoat, frilly white shirt, black stripy stockings and a huge, tri-cornered hat with a pink feather stuck in it. As he jauntily swung the ship's tiller this way and that, he hummed cheerfully to himself. Every now and again, he would also wobble his bottom saucily, and then do a frisky little dance, but only when he thought no one was watching. This was the *Grumpy Roger*'s captain. His name was Cornelius Codswallop.

Standing next to Captain Codswallop was a small, curly-haired boy aged about eleven. This was Norris, the *Grumpy Roger*'s cabin boy.

Beside Norris stood an even smaller red-haired man with a droopy, ginger moustache and an enormous, ginger beard. A green, checked bandana kept slipping over his eyes every time he moved his head. This was Horace Hale. But everyone called him Ginger Hale, because of his red hair. Ginger was Captain Codswallop's first mate (they'd been pals ever since they were both knee-high to a barnacle). Ginger was also first mate of the *Grumpy Roger*.

As Captain Codswallop, Norris and Ginger scanned the horizon and occasionally exchanged happy smiles, another ten pirates were busy doing all the stuff that pirates normally do. This included things like running up and down the rigging, picking the weevils out of their rations, picking their rations out of the weevils, pumping bilge, talking bilge, and taking turns to sit in the crows' nest (which, of course, annoyed the crows no end).

The pirates were on their way to a quayside tavern called the Dirty Duck. They were all in a really good mood, so they were singing their favourite song:

The pirate had a wooden leg

He called it Auntie Flo
And everywhere the pirate went
The leg was sure to go
Ho ho!

The reason the pirates were all feeling so happy was that a couple of days earlier they'd been sailing around looking for some mischief to get up to when they'd spotted a pair of magnificent, four-masted merchant ships parked in the Bay of Biscuits. After taking a long and careful look through his spyglass, Captain Codswallop had clapped a hand to his brow and cried, 'Well I'll be jiggered, lads! I can't see a single sailor aboard them there boats! I wonder where they all can be?'

'Look, cap'n!' Norris, the sharp-eyed cabin boy, had said. 'They're over there. In the sea. They're playing water polo!'

He was right. All the sailors were splashing about in the water playing a game with a large, white, minty sweet with a hole in the middle. Completely unaware that they were being spied on by the pirates, they laughed and shouted happily as they threw the sweet back and forth, all totally absorbed in their hilarious inter-ship polo match. It was too good an opportunity for the pirates to miss!

'Now, shipmates!' Captain Codswallop had said. 'I think it's time we went over there and took a look at what they've got on board them there merchant ships. From their posh looks, I suspect it might well be a prize worth taking. But we must do it very stealthily. We don't want to interrupt their little game, now do we? So remember, lads! No chin wagging, no whistling and definitely no yo-ho-hoing! And leave your parrots in their cages.'

At this, all the pirates had put their fingers on their lips and nodded, grinning with excitement and winking at each other mischievously. Then, setting off in a couple of rowing boats and taking great care not to make any big, noisy splashes with their oars, they'd rowed themselves over to the unguarded ships and climbed aboard.

To their absolute delight, they'd discovered that both ships were loaded with dozens of large chests, many of which looked as though they must certainly contain important and valuable cargo. As quickly and quietly as they could, the pirates had loaded the chests into their rowing boats, made their way back to the *Grumpy Roger*, and then headed for the horizon as quickly as they could!

As soon as they'd put a safe distance between themselves and the merchant ships, and Captain Codswallop was completely sure there was no chance of them being pursued, he'd ordered Ginger Hale to take over the tiller. Then he went below decks with the rest of the crew to inspect their booty.

'Right, lads!' Captain Codswallop had cried. 'It's time we took a little peep at today's pickings. Let's start with this here great big chest.'

The chest which the captain had chosen was secured with two huge padlocks, so it took him and the other pirates quite a long time to get it open. But the results were certainly well worth waiting for!

'Prancing porpoises and jitterbugging jelly fish!' cried Captain Codswallop, as he lifted the lid. 'Would you look at that!'

The crew took two paces back and gasped in awe! The chest was absolutely overflowing with glittering gold sovereigns and sparkling silver crowns! There must have been thousands and thousands of them!

'Phwoar!' cried the pirates. 'What a lot of dosh!'

'Ho, ho, lads!' cried Captain Codswallop. 'I think today must be our lucky day! And just to think, this is only the first chest! There are still lots more to open!' Then he paused, took a deep breath and said, 'You know what this means don't you, my hearties?'

'Yes, we do, Captain Codswallop!' cried the crew. 'We're rich beyond our wildest dreams!'

'We certainly are, my lads!' laughed Captain Codswallop. 'There's enough dosh in this here chest alone to keep every one of us in luxury parrots and designer swashbuckles for the rest of our lives! I think our stroke of fabulous good fortune calls for a celebration. Let's all go to the Dirty Duck and make merry. And let's not waste another second!'

So, without even taking the trouble to open the other chests, Captain Codswallop and his crew had set sail for Old London Town.

CHAPTER TWO

The *Grumpy Roger* had now almost reached the famous quayside tavern, and all along the riverbank people were looking alarmed and scrambling for cover.

'Look out, everyone!' yelled a grizzled, old seafarer. 'It's Captain Codswallop and the *Grumpy Roger*. He's about to dock. And we all know what he's like at parking! Oh no, would you look at that! He's heading straight for the jetty! There's bound to be an—'

All at once there was a horrible grinding noise and, the next moment, the *Grumpy Roger* crunched into the wooden landing jetty which jutted out from the quayside.

'—accident!' said the seafarer, as he toppled into the water.

Two seconds later, the entire jetty collapsed into the river in a shower of sticks and splinters. It was closely followed by the rest of the people who'd been standing on it!

'Who put that there?' yelled Captain Codswallop, as he watched the unfortunate folk tumble into the river. 'What a stupid place to leave a jetty!'

'You bungling buccaneer!' cried a sailor, as he thrashed about in the water. 'Why don't you look where you're going?'

'Yes, you feather-brained freebooter!' yelled his pal, as they doggy-paddled towards the quayside. 'You could have drowned the lot of us, you short-sighted, old swashbuckler, you!'

'Oh, stop complaining!' shouted Captain Codswallop. 'A drop of water never hurt anyone. Anyway, you two look like you could do with a bath!' Then he began wildly pushing the tiller this way and that as he yelled, 'I think I'll try reversing in this time, Ginger!'

Five minutes later, after lots more grinding, crunching, crashing and bashing, Captain Codswallop finally managed to steer the *Grumpy Roger* alongside the quay.

'Well done, captain!' cried Ginger Hale. 'You seem to be getting the hang of this parking lark at last! You only destroyed one jetty and six boats. And they were just titchy ones!'

'Shiver my shirt-tails and blast my braces,' roared Captain Codswallop. 'I've got us as snug as a tug in a jug! And bless my blithering britches, if we aren't almost in the front parlour of the Dirty Duck. You lot get in there and order up some grub 'n' grog. I'll just weigh the anchor.'

'Won't it weigh the same as it did last time, captain?' said Norris.

'Don't you try to tell me how to do my job, Norris my lad!' snarled Captain Codswallop. 'Or I'll give you a taste of the cat!'

Everyone went quiet. They hated it when the captain made them taste the cat.

So did the cat.

As Captain Codswallop was weighing the anchor, he listened to the happy singing of his crew coming from the front parlour of the Dirty Duck.

We're going to have a nosh up
We won't even have to wash up
Cos we can cough the dosh up
Ho ho!

'Well, they sound like they're having the time

15

of their life,' he said to himself. 'I'll just check that everything's shipshape before I go and join the party!'

Then, with a contented smile on his face, his hands on hips and his chest puffed out proudly, he stood back on the quayside and admired the *Grumpy Roger*.

There was no doubt about it. It was definitely shipshape. His old dad, Captain Cuthbert Codswallop, had taught him that he must always make sure that his boat was shipshape. He often wondered why.

After all, the *Grumpy Roger* isn't likely to have suddenly become carrot-shape ... or stagecoach-shape! he thought to himself.

As he clumped happily towards the tavern, Captain Codswallop was so busy sniggering at his little joke that he failed to notice the two sinister, masked figures who had just crept out of a dark alley and onto the quayside. They were now lurking in a shadowy doorway and eyeing Captain Codswallop and the *Grumpy Roger* very suspiciously indeed.

If Captain Codswallop had spotted them, he might have saved himself and his crew a great deal of trouble.

CHAPTER THREE

As soon as Captain Codswallop had disappeared into the Dirty Duck, the two masked figures emerged from the shadows and crept over to the *Grumpy Roger*.

'It's loads bigger than a stagecoach,' whispered the smaller one.

'Of course it's loads bigger than a stagecoach!' hissed the taller one. 'It's a blithering pirate ship … stupid!'

'We've never pinched a ship before, Dick,' said the small one. 'We've only pinched stagecoaches … and horses. I don't know how to ride a ship!'

'You don't ride it, Nick! You drive it. It's a boat!'

'Well, you can drive it, I'll trot along at the side.'

'You'd better be wearing your water wings then, Nick!' growled Dick. 'Now listen, it's not

18

as though we've got a choice! The queen's men have us surrounded. It'll only be a matter of minutes before they find us. Then we'll be for it! After what we've just gone and done, there's no telling what sort of horrid things they'll have lined up for us. But one thing's for sure: it'll most certainly end up with the pair us dangling from the gallows!'

'So, what you're saying, Dick, is that you're not to keen on hanging around!'

'Exactly!' replied Dick. 'And pinching this here ship is our only chance of escape. We'll sail it back up the Thames. Then, as soon as we get to Oxfordshire, we'll sell it.'

'What, Oxfordshire!?'

'No, the boat, blunder brains! We'll use the money to buy ourselves a couple of new horses. Before you know it, we'll be shouting "stand and deliver" again!'

'More like "stand in the river"' mumbled the small one.

In case you haven't realised by now, this was none other than the famous highwayman, Dick Turnip, and his somewhat less-famous, younger brother, Nick. They were in big trouble. Earlier that day they'd spotted a very grand-looking coach making its way through the English countryside. It was plain to see that it belonged to someone extremely wealthy and successful. So, of course, the Turnip brothers instantly realised that there were rich pickings to be had.

After quickly putting on their highwaymen masks, they'd taken a short cut across the fields in order get ahead of the coach and ambush it. Then, finding a good hiding place in some woods, they'd cocked their pistols, drawn their swords and prepared to relieve the coach's unsuspecting passengers of all their money and valuables.

The moment it had come clattering around a bend in the road, the two Turnips had galloped out of the trees, spurring their horses, wildly firing their pistols in the air and shouting things like, 'Give us yer dosh, Mr and Mrs Posh! We're the terrible Turnip brothers! We robs the snobs and we boffs the toffs!'

It was a pity that the Turnips hadn't looked a bit more carefully when they'd first spotted the coach. Unfortunately for them, they'd failed to realise that sitting inside the fabulous vehicle, was none other than Queen Elizabeth I of

England! The queen had been on her way to the Kent fishing port of Crabcake (later to be renamed Sandwich), with the intention of welcoming back her favourite, daredevil, globetrotting explorer, Sir Walter Raleigh.

Sir Walter had just returned from his three-month voyage to the New World where, amongst many other things, he'd discovered an exciting and wondrous new vegetable which he was going to be presenting to her when they met.

And, of course, people like the Queen of England don't go wandering around the dangerous, 16th-century English countryside without some sort of protection. Nor do they take kindly to being held up by common highwaymen. Not only did Queen Elizabeth have four huge bodyguards sitting next to her inside the coach but, galloping along a few hundred metres behind, and previously unseen by the Turnips, there were no less than 50 of her best fighting men. And they were all heavily armed.

So, as Dick and Nick had brought the coach to a halt with much shouting and sword waving, they got quite a surprise when the Queen of England stuck her head out of the window and yelled, 'You are so nicked! I'm the blinking Queen of England, I am! Yes, you most certainly chose the wrong coach this time, losers! Do you like dungeon food, or what?'

Then she'd screamed for her bodyguards to arrest the Turnips, take them to the Tower to suffer extremely painful and unspeakable things, before being strung up from the tallest gallows in Old London Town.

Dick and Nick had instantly realised that this would probably be something of an inconvenience, if not to say a complete pain in the neck. So they'd taken off in a cloud of dust and a screech of horseshoes, closely followed by the enormous royal posse.

After a long and hair-raising chase through the Kent countryside, with the queen's men hot on their heels, the brothers had finally reached the outskirts of Old London Town. However, by this time, the two Turnips' horses were so exhausted by the chase that, on arriving at the city gates, they'd simply sat down in the middle of the road and wouldn't run any further. Dick and Nick had immediately fallen to their knees and begged their steeds to go on just a bit further. However, despite the brothers making all manner of promises, including mountains of sugar lumps and buckets of carrots, the horses had simply turned their backs on them and refused to budge another inch.

So the Turnips had had no choice but to abandon their mounts and dash into the city, desperately hoping that they might lose their pursuers in the maze of lanes and alleys that made up Old London Town. But the brothers were unfamiliar with the twists and turns of the capital. And the queen's men were very, very determined! Especially as Queen Elizabeth had promised a reward of ten gold sovereigns to each of them for successfully bringing in one of the most notorious highwaymen in England, dead or alive!

After a terrifying game of cat and mouse, which involved lots of running in and out of taverns, shops and alleyways, the soldiers had finally chased the Turnips down to the quayside. Now, having got them surrounded, they were closing in on them. The brothers were going to have to make a quick decision if they wanted to live to rob another day.

'Come on then. Let's get on with it!' said Dick, as he threw away his mask and dragged Nick up the gangplank of the *Grumpy Roger*. 'We'll check round to make sure the pirates haven't left a guard, and then we'll be off. Look, those stupid swashbucklers were in such a hurry to get into the pub that they didn't even bother to take down the sails. I've got a feeling this whole thing's going to be a piece of cake!

The Turnips didn't have to worry about a guard being on the *Grumpy Roger*. The whole crew was in the Dirty Duck having a fine old time, laughing like drains and slapping each

24

other on the back, still unable to believe their fabulous good fortune, as they played Pin the Tail on the Mermaid.

As the two highwaymen wandered about the deserted ship, Dick spotted a sign which read: Before Leaving Port Always Weigh the Anchor!

He and his brother immediately hauled up the anchor and staggered around below deck looking for some scales. While they were doing this, a stiff breeze sprang up and the tide turned, causing the *Grumpy Roger* to drift rapidly out to sea!

CHAPTER FOUR

As the customs house clock struck nine, the pirates charged out of the Dirty Duck. Captain Codswallop pushed past his men and dashed off into the darkness, shouting, 'Last one on the *Grumpy Roger*'s a sissy!'

Suddenly there was a huge splash.

'Where's the captain gone?' cried Ginger Hale.

There was another splash.

'Where's Ginger gone?' cried Norris.

There was yet another splash.

'Where's Norris gone?' cried the rest of the crew.

There were lots more splashes.

'Where's the *Grumpy Roger* gone?' cried everyone, as they thrashed about in the icy water of the River Thames.

Ten minutes later, the pirates were back in the Dirty Duck standing around the fire in their wet undies and shivering with cold. They were all feeling very, very miserable indeed.

'We're in a predicament now, shipmates!' groaned Captain Codswallop. 'No *Grumpy Roger*, no chests of treasure, no nothing … we're sunk!'

'It's no good standing about feeling sorry for ourselves, cap'n,' said Norris. 'We'll just have to get another boat and chase after those thieves!'

'That won't be as easy as it sounds,' said Captain Codswallop. 'All the boats parked round here have guards on board.'

'Apart from the *Grumpy Roger*,' mumbled Norris. 'More's the pity!'

'What did you just say?' said Captain Codswallop.

'Err, "What a wicked city!" ' piped up Norris.

'You can say that again!' muttered Captain Codswallop.

At that moment, the door of the Dirty Duck opened and a disgusting smell wafted in. It was followed by an extremely tubby man carrying a basket of rotting fish. He was wearing a floppy, leather hat, a long, greasy overcoat and a black mask, and he was shouting, 'Get yer kippers! Get yer fish fingers! Get yer lobsters' armpits!'

'Well, bless my bulkhead and shiver my shorelines, it's my old pal, Smelly Fisher!' cried Captain Codswallop, hardly able to believe his eyes. 'How you doin' Smelly, my old fishfurter?'

'I be doin' just fine Cap'n Codswallop!' cried Smelly. 'Long time, no sea! Ho! Ho!'

'Ho! Ho!' laughed the captain. 'That's right, Smelly! Long time, no sea! Now, what's that there mask thing you're wearin'?'

'This be a mask thing what I just found on the quayside,' said Smelly. He stuck a crab claw in the captain's ribs and shouted, 'Now I be one of them there highwaymen. Stick up yer mitts and stand on yer liver! Ho! Ho! Ho!'

'Ho! Ho! Ho!' laughed Captain Codswallop, really getting into the spirit of things and throwing his arms in the air, as he pretended to be Smelly's terrified victim.

'Ho! Ho! Ho!' shouted the pirates, all thoroughly enjoying the joke.

'Ho! Ho! Ho! Got you at last, you horrid highwayman!' shouted the queen's Sergeant at Arms, as he and his men rushed into the Dirty Duck and pounced on Smelly.

'Oh no!' groaned Norris, as he saw what was happening.

Then, as Captain Codswallop and his crew watched in horror and disbelief, six enormous soldiers pushed Smelly up against the wall and began to clamp him in chains.

'Dick Turnip!' roared the Sergeant at Arms. 'Just two hours ago, you and your evil accomplice attempted to hold up a coach containing no lesser person that Her Royal Self, Queen Elizabeth I of England!'

'Sergeant!' cried Captain Codswallop, truly shocked at what was happening to his friend. 'I swear on my grandpa's wooden teeth! That's not Dick Turnip. It's my old pal, Smelly Fisher, I've known him for years!'

'You stay out of this you interfering, old buccaneer!' barked the Sergeant at Arms. 'Or I'll have you clapped in irons, too!' Then, he turned to Smelly and said, 'Dick Turnip, I am now arresting you in the name of Good Queen Bess! And I also demand to know the whereabouts of your horrible little brother?'

'I ain't got no blinking little brother!' yelled Smelly. 'I've only got my sister Shirley what sells seashells on the seashore!'

'A likely story, Turnip!' roared the Sergeant at Arms. 'But no matter, we'll soon hunt down your wicked brother and bring him to justice, too. In the meantime you will be taken to the Tower of London and brought before Her Majesty. Then, wearing your highwayman's mask, you will be made to shout, "We're the terrible Turnip brothers! We robs the snobs and we boffs the toffs!" And if she identifies you as one of the men who robbed her coach, you will immediately have your gimlets scrimbled!

Then you will have your crottle thrimped! And finally you will be made to sit on the scrawky board! And it will jolly well serve you right. You wicked scoundrel, you!'

'But ... but ... I'm not Dick Turnip,' protested Smelly. 'I be Smelly!'

'Phwoar! You can say that again,' said the soldiers, as they marched him out of the tavern.

'Poor old Smelly,' said the pirates, looking more miserable than ever. 'Fancy him having his crottle thrimped!'

'Just the thought of sitting on that blinking scrawky board makes my eyes water,' said Ginger Hale. Then he paused and added, 'By the way, what is a scrawky board?'

'Not the foggiest!' said the rest of the pirates, with a shrug of their shoulders.

'Oh dear,' said Captain Codswallop. 'I hope they don't do anything really horrible to him!'

'I wouldn't worry too much,' said Norris with a twinkle in his eye. 'They'll probably set him free when the queen realises he's not a Turnip.'

Then he sidled up to Captain Codswallop, gently elbowed him in the ribs and whispered, 'And in the meantime, cap'n, old Smelly will be needing someone to look after his boat, won't he?'

'Norris!' said Captain Codswallop, with a huge grin. 'You took the words right out of my brain!'

•

It didn't take the pirates long to find Smelly's boat. They simply followed their noses to the battered, old wreck that had the words the *Flying Kipper* painted on the side. To their dismay, the whole boat was overflowing with fish of every shape and size. And quite a few of them were very old and very smelly!

'This be it then, my hearties,' said the captain as they clambered aboard.

'Poooo! Coor! What a pong!' groaned the pirates, sliding about on the slippery deck and holding their noses.

'Surely you're not planning to put to sea with that lot on board?' said Norris.

'Oh, I don't know,' said Captain Codswallop. 'They aren't such a bad crowd when you get to know them. T'would be a shame to go without them.'

'I don't mean the pirates, cap'n. I mean the fish!' said Norris.

'Oh, I see what you mean. Well there's no time to unload them now,' said Captain Codswallop. 'The sooner we catch those rascals who stole our ship ... the better!'

CHAPTER FIVE

'The sooner we get to Oxford, the better!' thought Dick Turnip as he clung to the tiller of the *Grumpy Roger* and watched the banks of the River Thames slide past. It was now daylight and they seemed to have covered miles. Dick hadn't realised that sailing ships could travel so fast.

The wind was driving the *Grumpy Roger* along so swiftly that his knuckles were beginning to turn white as he tried to keep it on course. Steering a pirate ship was really hard work! No matter how many he times he clicked his tongue and cried, 'Whoa, Grumpy boy! Whoa!' Dick just couldn't get the ship to slow down or go in a straight line. He'd even tried flicking his riding whip in an effort to make the *Grumpy Roger* behave. But it didn't make the slightest bit of difference. For the last half an hour or so, the ship had been swerving wildly from one bank of the river to the other, as the farm workers in the surrounding fields dropped their hoes and watched, open-mouthed in amazement.

Dick wouldn't have felt quite such an idiot if the *Grumpy Roger* hadn't been going backwards! But, no matter how energetically he moved the tiller, he simply couldn't get the ship to point in the right direction. And, to make matters worse, the river was now getting really, really busy. There were fishing boats returning to port with their catches, barges full of wood and coal, merchant ships loaded with silks and spices and market-bound river ferries criss-crossing the channels with their noisy cargoes of pigs, sheep and chickens.

Dick was desperately looking over his shoulder as he frantically swung the tiller this way and that in a last-minute attempt to avoid colliding with all these rivercraft, not to mention the islands which were looming up with alarming speed. He wished his brother was around to help him keep a look out for obstacles. But the moment Nick had realised the *Grumpy Roger* was on the move, he'd dashed below deck like a frightened rabbit.

Every now and again he would shout up,

'Are we there yet?' and Dick would reply, 'Nearly, Nick! I've almost got the hang of this ship-driving lark. Once I find the reins, it'll be a piece of cake!'

Which wasn't true at all. Dick wasn't even sure they were going in the right direction. He was sure rivers were supposed to get narrower as you went inland. But this one was getting wider! And wider! After a while he couldn't see the banks. And there seemed to be seabirds everywhere!

Suddenly, Dick spotted a small fishing village on an island in the middle of the river. They were heading straight for it! Giving way to terror and panic, he took his hands off the tiller and covered his eyes, expecting to be smashed to smithereens at any moment! But then, to his enormous relief, he felt the *Grumpy Roger* begin to turn! And all at once, for the first time since they'd left Old London Town, the ship was facing in the right direction! And then it wasn't! And then it was! And then it wasn't!

After a few moments of confusion, Dick realised what was happening. The *Grumpy Roger* was now spinning like a cork in a whirlpool! As the powerful current twirled them past the fishing village, he spotted a crowd of fisher-folk staring in amazement at his astonishing, revolving pirate ship. They were cheering and hooting with laughter but, above the sound of their shrieks and catcalls, Dick could hear a horrible groaning sound. Looking in the direction of the noise, he spotted Nick hanging over the front end of the boat. His face was as green as the paint on the *Grumpy Roger*'s woodwork.

'I feel sick, Dick,' he moaned. 'Stop the ship, Dick!'

'Goodness gracious me!' yelled an old sailor on the quayside. 'It's a talking figurehead!'

'No, I'm not!' groaned Nick. 'I'm Nick! And I feel sick. Stop the ship, Dick!'

'Stop the ship for Nick, Dick!' chorused the crowd on the banks, who were now enjoying themselves hugely. 'You better be quick, Dick! He's going to be sick, Dick!'

The teasing and the twirling were more than the two Turnip brothers could bear. Both of them were now beginning to wish that they were back at the Tower of London, about to have their gimlets scrimbled. But there was no chance of that! The current was now sweeping them past the island and out into a huge expanse of open water.

'Was that Oxford?' groaned Nick, as he looked back at the fishing village.

'Err, yes I think so.' said Dick.

'Then why did it have that big sign saying "Last Ship's Biscuits Before The English Channel"?' said Nick.

CHAPTER SIX

Once the crew of the *Grumpy Roger* had tidied the fish into piles and given the deck of the *Flying Kipper* a quick scrub, they were ready to set off in search of their stolen boat. But, of course, the first thing they had to do was find out which way it had gone. They were in luck! After spending a few moments questioning people on the quayside, they came across a night watchman who said he was sure he had seen the *Grumpy Roger* heading east.

'In other words, towards the open sea!' exclaimed Captain Codswallop. 'I wonder what those ship-lifting bilge-buckets can be up to? Right, let's get after them, lads!'

And with that, they upped anchor, hoisted the *Flying Kipper's* one and only, extremely threadbare, sail and set off towards the Thames Estuary.

Despite its name, the *Flying Kipper* was not

built for speed, and progress was slow, much to the frustration of Captain Codswallop and his men. However, just as the sun was peeping over the eastern horizon they reached some water meadows a few miles beyond London, where they spotted a farm boy leading a horse and cart along the riverbank.

Captain Codswallop decided to ask him if he'd seen anything of the *Grumpy Roger*.

'Ahoy there, little landlubber!' he called, as he steered the *Flying Kipper* alongside the lad. 'I've lost a pirate ship. It's a big, green wooden thing; answers to the name of the *Grumpy Roger*! Have you seen it?'

'Phwoar!' cried the lad, grabbing his nose. 'You're a mongy lote ob birats, aren't you! Det, ad a batter of fat, I tid dee a birat jip. It went dit way! An' dat way! Den dit way again! An' it wad going bakwuds aw de dime!'

'Add a batter of fat? Dit way? Dat way?' said Captain Codswallop, looking at Norris in bewilderment. 'They don't half talk funny round here, don't they, Norris? Or do you think the poor little twit's got a jib loose?'

'He's holding his nose because he can't stand the smell of our fish!' said Norris. 'I think what he's saying is something like, "Yes, as matter of fact I did see a pirate ship. It went dit way! An' dat way! And it was going backwards aw de dime!" Or something like that?'

'Dat way? Dit way? Backwards?' exclaimed Captain Codswallop. 'That sounds very odd. The *Grumpy's* normally such a well-behaved little boat. I hope it isn't being mistreated!'

'Well, at least we know that those boatnappers haven't skedaddled off up a tributary and hidden themselves away,' said Norris. 'So we're most definitely still going in the right direction.'

'Yes, that's true!' said Captain Codswallop. 'Thank you very much, little country pumpkin! Throw him a fish for his breakfast, Norris.'

When they reached the fishing village on the island, Captain Codswallop spotted the sailor who'd mistaken Nick for a figurehead and called, 'Ahoy there, matey, have you been here long?'

'Yes, I have, shipmate!' replied the old sea dog. 'About 98 years!'

'In that case you might be able to help us,' called Captain Codswallop. 'We're looking for a big, green pirate ship. It was probably going backwards.'

'Oh, I seen that!' said the old chap. 'But it weren't going backwards. It were twirling. Like this!'

He began to whirl along the quayside but, after a moment or so, he appeared to go dizzy and flopped down on a mooring post, looking really pale and ill.

'That reminds me!' he said. 'It had a talking figurehead, with a green face, which kept groaning and moaning. And the captain was shouting "Whoa!" and "Giddyup!" and larruping the deck with his cat o' one tail.'

'His cat o' one tail?' said Captain Codswallop, looking puzzled. 'What's one of them when it's at home?'

'I think he means a whip, Captain Codswallop,' said Norris. 'It sounds like this chap was probably lashing the *Grumpy Roger* with a whip.'

'The scoundrel!' yelled Captain Codswallop. 'I'll give him a whip! Just wait till I get my mitts on him!' Then he turned back to the old man and cried, 'Did you get the name?'

'Yes, it were Dick,' shouted the old chap. 'The talking figurehead called him Dick!'

'No, not *his* name, you batty old barnacle!' yelled Captain Codswallop. 'The *boat's* name!'

'There's no need to be rude!' said the old sailor. 'I'm doing my best. I am 98 you know!'

'Sorry about that,' said Captain Codswallop. 'I didn't mean to be rude. It's because I'm feeling so upset about losing the—'

'*Grumpy Roger!*' said the old man.

'How did you know that?' exclaimed Captain Codswallop.

'It said so on the side,' said the old man.

CHAPTER SEVEN

Half an hour later, the *Flying Kipper* sailed out of the Thames Estuary and into the English Channel. Then, twenty minutes after that, to the utter disappointment of Captain Codswallop and his crew, the wind dropped and a thick fog came down. All at once the sail of the *Flying Kipper* began to droop like a wet dishcloth. And so did the crew!

'Well, that's that, then!' groaned Captain Codswallop. 'We're becalmed. We can't go another mile. We've lost our beloved *Grumpy Roger*.'

'And all those chests full of lovely money,' Norris added gloomily. 'We'll never catch up with them now.'

For a few moments the crew stood around staring at their feet and sighing in despair, but then Ginger Hale began jumping up and down and yelled, 'I've just a had an idea! Why don't we get out and push?'

'Just what I was thinking!' exclaimed Captain Codswallop. 'You're a genius, Ginger!' Then he turned to the crew and said, 'OK, you lot! Get out and push. I'll steer. You be the lookout, Norris. And you can be the foghorn, Ginger.

Ginger grinned from ear to ear, then went, '*Beep, beep, beeeeeeep!*'

But the crew all looked really unhappy and grumbled something about not having their swimming trunks with them and the water being too cold. Then they began to mutter rebelliously.

'Oh dear, I hope there isn't going to be a mutterny!' said Captain Codswallop.

'Don't worry, cap'n!' said Norris. 'I know what to do.' Then he whispered something in his ear and a huge grin spread across Captain Codswallop's face.

'Shipmates!' he cried. 'I've just had yet another brilliant idea. As a special favour I've decided that I'm going to allow you all to keep your clothes on when you get into the water. That way you'll stay nice and warm!'

'Phwoar, captain, you ain't half clever!' said the crew. 'Why didn't we think of that?'

'I'm not captain for nothing, you know,'

said Captain Codswallop, as he watched them all throw themselves into the sea.

'*Beep, beep, beeeeep!*' went Ginger Hale.

'Left hand down a bit. Right hand up a bit!' called Norris. 'No, not you, Ginger. I'm talking to the captain!'

But Norris was wasting his time. What with all the excitement from the previous day and the sleepless night that had followed the theft of the *Grumpy Roger*, Captain Codswallop was utterly pooped. And more to the point he wasn't doing his duty by standing at the tiller and attempting to steer the *Flying Kipper* through the treacherous fog banks. Instead, he was fast asleep, curled up in a ball on the deck with his thumb in his mouth, chuckling to himself and grinning like an idiot as he dreamed of piratical adventures past.

In fact, Captain Codswallop was in such a deep and peaceful sleep that he hadn't even noticed when a gentle breeze had sprung up about twenty minutes earlier and begun to push the *Flying Kipper* further out into the English Channel. But the crew certainly had! With a cry of, 'Thank goodness for that!' they'd instantly clambered back on board and quickly got themselves warm and dry again by running around the deck a couple of times and then wrapping themselves in blankets. And they, too, were now fast asleep in their hammocks. The only two people who had managed to stay awake were Norris and Ginger.

As Ginger continued to beep happily, Norris was doing his best to stay alert and work out where they actually were, despite being just as tired as everyone else. From what he could gather, he guessed they were still somewhere quite near the south coast of England. However, in spite of the breeze, the fog was as thick as ever, so he couldn't be absolutely certain. All he knew was that their chances of ever seeing the *Grumpy Roger* again were getting less by the second.

But then, just as he was gently shaking Captain Codswallop by the shoulder and attempting to wake him for the third time, the fog lifted slightly. Peering through the thinning murk, Norris saw something that made his heart race and his pulse throb! Looming up out of the gloom was a large ship-shaped silhouette! And it was heading straight for the *Flying Kipper*!

'Ship ahoy!' yelled Norris, giving his captain one last almighty shake. 'Wake up, cap'n! Wake up!'

Captain Codswallop twitched twice, then leapt to his feet and began running around the deck like a headless chicken, yelling, 'No problem, Norris. I've got everything completely under control. Now, where did I put that blithering tiller?'

But it was too late. A moment later there was a sickening crunch and the two ships collided.

'*Beep ... beep*?' said Ginger Hale.

'Juddering jellyfish!' roared Captain Codswallop. 'What on ocean is going on?'

'We've crashed,' said Norris.

'Crashed?' cried Captain Codswallop. 'How could we have crashed? I've been at the tiller all the time!' Then he peered into the gloom and shouted, 'Ahoy, you over there, you've just crashed into our blinking boat!'

'Sorry about that,' replied a strange voice through the fog. 'It's this pea soup. I can't see a thing in it.'

'You shouldn't be eating pea soup at a time like this!' yelled Captain Codswallop. 'You should be watching where you're going. Just like I was!'

'I *was* watching where I was going!' replied the voice. 'I was talking about the fog. It's like pea soup. You know ... thick!'

'Don't you call me thick!' shouted Captain Codswallop. 'Or I'll come over there and box your ears!'

'You obviously haven't the foggiest what I'm talking about!' said the voice.

'You can say that again!' said Captain Codswallop. 'I'm completely mystified. Anyway, where are you going?'

'We're looking for Oxfordshire,' said the voice. 'You haven't seen it, have you?'

'No, we haven't,' said Captain Codswallop. 'We're busy looking for our ship, the *Grumpy Roger*. Some scoundrels stole it while we were in a pub in Old London Town. I mean, what's the world coming to when a bunch of hard-working pirates can't leave their ship unattended for a few minutes without someone trying to nick it?'

'Don't blame me!' said another voice. 'It wasn't my idea!'

'Shut up, Nick!' said the first voice. 'He wasn't talking about you.'

'Anyway,' continued Captain Codswallop. 'If those boat thieves knew what we're going to do with them when we get hold of them, their teeth would knock and their knees would chatter! For starters we're going to mince their scallops. Really, *really* slowly. And then we'll crush their spangles! One at a time! And after that we'll probably pull off their—'

'Ooer!' said the second voice. 'I don't like the sound of this one bit, Dick. I've come over all of a tremble!'

'Here, what's that jingling noise?' said Captain Codswallop.

'Keep your knees still, Nick!' whispered the first voice. 'And if you can't stop them knocking, at least take off your spurs! You mustn't panic! As long as this fog stays down, we're fine. Ooer, it's blinking-well lifting!'

It was true. The fog was lifting and thinning again. And, in just a few more seconds, it had cleared enough for Captain Codswallop and his men to see the battered, green pirate ship, which was rocking gently on the waves just a few metres away from the *Flying Kipper*.

'By the cringe!' roared Captain Codswallop, as he caught sight of the *Grumpy Roger*. 'There's my ship!'

Standing at the tiller of the *Grumpy* was a tall figure wearing a long, black cape and holding a riding whip. Next to it was a smaller one wearing a black mask and holding its knees. But then the fog fell again and the ship disappeared.

Captain Codswallop turned to his crew and yelled, 'Did you just see what I saw?'

'Yes, we did!' roared the crew. 'We saw our lovely *Grumpy Roger*! And the two scoundrels who nicked it!'

'Well, let's get after them then!' yelled the captain. 'Which way did they go?'

'I'm not sure?' said Ginger Hale. 'Do you want me to beep?'

'No, of course I don't want you to beeping-well beep, you daft little beeper! I want you to tell me where my ship is!'

Once more, the swirling mist lifted slightly and the *Grumpy Roger* became visible through the gloom.

'Err, there they are, over there,' shrieked Ginger. '*Beep! Beep! Beep!*'

'Oh, yes, so they are! Well spotted, Ginger!' yelled Captain Codswallop, after a couple of seconds. 'After them, lads!'

As the *Flying Kipper* drew near the *Grumpy Roger* again, Captain Codswallop waved his cutlass in the air and yelled, 'Look lively, you loathsome, lily-livered lickspittles! We're going to board you. And then we'll—'

Captain Codswallop's sentence was suddenly cut short by a huge explosion. It was closely followed by a terrifying, whistling sound. And a split-second later a cannonball knocked Captain Codswallop's cutlass right out of his hand and into the sea!

CHAPTER EIGHT

'Lolloping lobsters and lugubrious limpets!' yelled Captain Codswallop. 'Where did that come from?'

But, before anyone could answer, a second explosion rang out and another cannonball dropped into the sea right next to the *Flying Kipper*.

'Manky mermaids and shuffling sea legs!' roared the captain. 'Those blithering boat burglars are shooting at us. Man the guns!'

'We haven't got any guns,' said Norris. 'We're a fishing boat!'

'Well, man the fish then!' shouted the captain. 'Man the nets! Man anything!'

There was another explosion and a third cannonball whizzed past the captain's ear, taking one of his gi-normous earrings with it!

'Snivelling sandhoppers!' he cried. 'Did you see that? It took the earring right out of my ear!'

'It's put an eery ringing into my ear!' said Norris. 'That explosion was massive. I'd never realised the *Grumpy Roger*'s guns were so powerful!'

'It's taken the hearing right out my ear!' said Ginger. 'I'm half-deaf now!'

'In that case you'll be needing this!' said Norris, and he pushed a fish into Ginger's ear hole.

'What is it?' said Ginger.

'A herring aid!' said Norris.

There was another explosion.

'Cripes!' said Norris. 'That one came from behind us. You know what this means, don't you, cap'n?'

'Yes!' yelled Captain Codswallop. 'It means them there boat thieves are doing some pretty fancy shooting!'

'No, it doesn't,' said Norris. 'It means there's more than one of them!'

'Don't be silly, Norris!' laughed the captain. 'How on ocean can there be two *Grumpy Rogers*? I'm the captain! And there's only one of me, isn't there?'

A third cannonball whizzed over their heads. This one came from yet another direction!

'There won't be for much longer, if you don't keep your head down!' yelled Norris. 'Now do you see what I mean? That cannonball came from over there. So that means there must be at least three of them!'

'Surely they can't all be *Grumpy Rogers*?' said Captain Codswallop.

'No, cap'n! They're not! But I think I know what's happened!' said Norris. 'Whoever nicked the *Grumpy Roger* must have joined up with some other ships. Probably the rest of their gang. And now they're all attacking us!'

'Look, captain!' yelled Ginger Hale, pointing towards a line of huge ships, which were now partly visible through the swirling fog. 'None of them are *Grumpy Rogers*! They're all far too big!'

'Well, if they aren't the *Grumpy Roger*, where can our ship have got to?' said Captain Codswallop.

At that moment, something wooden and ship-shaped bumped into the *Flying Kipper*.

'Oops, sorry about that!' said a voice. 'I just can't see a thing in this fog. We're looking for Oxfordshire. You haven't seen it anywhere, have you?'

'It's them! The ship-nappers!' cried Captain Codswallop. 'Don't let them get away!'

'It's all right, captain!' yelled Ginger Hale. 'I've got hold of the *Grumpy*'s deck rail. They won't get away so easily this time. Oh no! We're drifting apart!'

It was true! The two boats were drifting apart and poor Ginger was now hanging on for dear life!

'Don't lose your grip, Ginger, you brave little nitwit!' cried Captain Codswallop.

'It's his feet, cap'n!' cried Norris. 'Look, they're lifting off the deck!'

'Grab hold of them then, Norris!' cried the captain. 'If he stays like that a few seconds longer, I can use him as a bridge to cross over onto my ship. You don't mind me walking over you, do you, Ginger?'

'Be my guest, captain!' cried brave Ginger. 'You can depend on me! I'm as thick as two planks you know. Norris told me so, only the other day!'

A second later, Captain Codswallop scrambled onto the deck rail and began to edge across Ginger's back, arms stretched out, balancing like a tightrope walker. But, as the two ships drifted even further apart, the plucky little first mate finally lost his grip on the *Grumpy Roger* and was left dangling upside down, five metres above the sea. And, just as he did, Captain Codswallop made a dramatic leap to land safely aboard the *Grumpy Roger*. Or, to be more exact, aboard Nick Turnip.

'Oh, Dick!' cried Nick. 'I've been hit by an enormous, squidgy cannonball!'

'Less of the squidgy!' growled Captain Codswallop. Then he looked down at Nick and roared, 'Anyway, I've got you now, you sneaky little ship-shifter!'

He staggered to his feet, took hold of the terrified highwayman by the scruff of his neck and the seat of his pants, then lifted him high above his head and began to spin him around.

'Now, I'll show you what *us pirates* do with boat thieves!' he roared. 'We'll start with a typhoon twizzler! Then I'll give you a shark's cuddle!'

Ignoring his brother's squeaks of terror, Dick Turnip stepped forwards and held out his hand to Captain Codswallop. 'How do you do?' he said, as cool as a sea cucumber. 'I'm Dick Turnip, the famous highwayman. How nice of you to drop in on us. I do hope you didn't mind us borrowing your boat. We were rather desperate, you see. Had a bit of a misunderstanding with the queen and her bodyguards. And, of course, we were most definitely intending to return it to you, once we'd put a safe distance between ourselves and our pursuers. By the way, the little chap you're now smothercating is my slightly less-famous brother. I'll introduce you properly, if you put him down.'

All at once there were more explosions and the air was suddenly thick with cannonballs again.

'You tell your pals to stop shooting and I'll put him down!' growled Captain Codswallop.

'What pals?' said Dick.

'Your pals over there, of course!' said the captain. 'That lot in those great, big ships.'

'They're nothing to do with us!' said Dick. 'We thought they were with you! They've been shooting at us as well, you know!'

'Well, if they're not with you and they're not with us, who are they with?' roared Captain Codswallop.

'They're with the King of Spain!' yelled Norris, as he steered the *Flying Kipper* alongside the *Grumpy Roger*. 'Look!'

Captain Codswallop dropped Nick Turnip on the deck and gazed around him. The sun had just broken through the fog and, for the first time, it was possible to see for more than a few metres. He gasped in astonishment. The *Grumpy Roger* and the *Flying Kipper* were completely surrounded by a vast fleet of massive warships. There were dozens and dozens of them stretching all the way to the horizon! And they were all bristling with cannon, while their decks seethed with thousands of soldiers and sailors.

'Well I'll fry a wooden leg in butter and serve it with a squeeze of lemon!' cried Captain Codswallop. 'I've never seen anything like this before! There must be hundreds of ships out there!'

'And they're all flying the Spanish flag,' said Norris, as he scrambled aboard the *Grumpy Roger*. 'We must have sailed in amongst them under cover of the fog!'

'But why have they been shooting at us?' said the captain. 'We aren't at war with Spain? We're at war with the French!'

61

'No, the war with the French was at least a fortnight ago,' said Dick Turnip. 'Last week we were at war with the Dutch, but this week it's the Spaniards!'

'He's right you know, cap'n!' said Norris. 'I overheard the landlord talking about it in the Dirty Duck last night. Queen Bess has been sending the King of Spain bananas and he's been sending her nuts. They're mad about each other. He wants to show her how tough he is. So that's probably why this lot are here. Look, the important-looking bloke on the really big boat is waving at us. I think he's going to say something.'

CHAPTER NINE

'Good mornings, Hinglishmens! My name is Don Alfonso De Torremolinos. I ham admireable of the meaty Spinach flea!' shouted the important-looking man who was standing on the bridge of the biggest Spanish galleon. He had a pointy, black beard and was wearing a big hat with a feather in it.

'Admireable of the meaty Spinach flea?' said Captain Codswallop. 'What on ocean is that when it's at home?'

'He's saying he's the admiral of the mighty Spanish fleet, cap'n!' explained Norris. 'It's all those ships you can see over there! They're the Spanish Armada!'

'I didn't know you could speak Spanish!' said the captain.

'I can't!' said Norris

'So this is the famous Hinglish Navvy!' shouted Admiral Torremolinos, waving his hand scornfully in the direction of the *Flying Kipper* and the *Grumpy Roger*. 'And I is presumings you is Sir Fancy Drinks and Sir Water Drily, the famous squash-bottlers who we har hallways earrings about.'

'It's swashbucklers, actually!' called Norris.

'Well I ham tellings you this!' continued the admiral. 'Your squash-bottling days is over. Your flock of sheeps is blinkings pathetics! Is this the bests you can be doings? It is a very comicackle thing to see! My sailors are being tittered pink by the lookings of it. They are havings the screamings abs dabs. Listens!'

Captain Codswallop and the crew listened. They could hear roars of laughter drifting over the water from the Spanish fleet.

'And I will tell you what we have been doings while we have been taking the potty shotty at you!'

'What have you been doing?' shouted Captain Codswallop.

'We have been putting our eyes in our jellyslops!'

'That's disgusting!'

'I think he means their telescopes, cap'n,' said Norris.

'Hand we have been peepings at your little bots!' continued the admiral.

'You rude lot!' exclaimed Captain Codswallop.

'And I am toldings you,' continued Admiral Torremolinos. 'We have never seen such pathetics little bots in our whole life. We are so tittered pinks that we are all beings the gigglings Gerties.'

'You ought to be ashamed of yourselves!' said Dick Turnip.

'Listen, Sir Fancy Drinks and Sir Water Drily!' continued Admiral Torremolinos.

'Spinach bots are big bots! And my bot is the biggest of them all. When I am sailing into the arbours, all the peoples is gaspings and pointings and saying, "Cor, just look at Admireable Don Alfonso Torremolinos's lovely big bot! It is the most hugest and most beautifulest bot I ever did see. Such a lovely shape and pretty colours! Oh, I am really wishings I ad a big lovely bot like that!"'

'He's a very rude man, isn't he, Norris?' said Captain Codswallop. 'He can't stop talking about bottoms!'

'I think he means boats actually, cap'n,' said Norris.

'Oh, I see! I see!' said the captain.

'Si, si!' said the Spanish admiral. 'We have got the biggest bots and we have got you surrendered. Your Hinglish Navvy must now be surroundering! Hand over your sheeps!'

'We haven't got any sheep?' said the captain,

'He means ships,' said Norris. 'I think they want us to hand over the *Flying Kipper* and the *Grumpy Roger*.'

'Snivelling shrimps and prancing prawns! Not on my granny's whalebone hip, I'm not!' thundered Captain Codswallop. 'We've only just got our *Grumpy Roger* back and I'm certainly not going to hand it over to that lot.' He suddenly lowered his voice and added, 'Especially with all that treasure on board. Tell him he's got enough ships as it is! Tell him to go and pick on someone his own size!'

'It will probably mean a fight, cap'n,' whispered Norris.

'I don't care!' roared the captain. 'We'll fight then. Draw the fleet into battle formation. Let the Spanish Armada do its worst! Now, where did I put my cutlass?'

•

Captain Codswallop had just enough time to tie the *Flying Kipper* to the stern of the *Grumpy Roger* and swear in the Turnip brothers as trainee pirates before the battle began. With only two small boats and 14 men under his command, he was somewhat outnumbered by the mighty Spanish war fleet, so he was really glad of the help from the highwaymen. Even so, the whole battle would probably have all been over in jiffy, if it hadn't been for the return of the fog.

'Thank goodness for that!' said Norris, as he tottered across the deck with a cannonball. 'These fog banks will be perfect cover for us.

And there's still a bit of a breeze. We'll be able to nip in and out of the mist patches and keep the Spaniards guessing!'

'Ooh! Are we going to play hide and seek?' said Ginger excitedly. 'I love hide and seek! Bags I be on first!'

'All right then, Ginger, you can be on first!' said Norris. 'Now listen carefully! These are the rules. Take the rowing boat and head for England. Then, when you see a large fleet of English warships, tell them about this big game of hide and seek we're playing with the Spanish Armada and ask them if they want to come and play, too! Have you got that?'

Ginger nodded enthusiastically and immediately set off in the rowing boat.

'And remember not to beep!' shouted Norris.

CHAPTER TEN

The battle between the pirates and the Spanish Armada soon began to hot up and in no time at all the air was thick with smoke and salty curses, as one cannonball after another plopped harmlessly into the sea. Norris's 'miss and run' plan was definitely keeping the *Grumpy Roger* out of the Armada's way.

Every time one of the galleons appeared out of the gloom, the pirates would fire a quick blast from one of their cannons. Then, after pulling some really silly faces at the enemy, they would scurry back into the cover of the fog.

'If we can keep this up until help arrives, we'll be all right!' shouted Captain Codswallop, as they hid in a fog bank for the umpteenth time that day.

'There's only one problem though!' replied Norris.

'What's that then?' said the captain.

'We're almost out of ammunition!' said Norris. 'We're down to our last two cannonballs!'

'Pithering pilchards!' exclaimed the captain. 'We mustn't let them know that, or we're sunk! We'll just have to throw everything we've got! Use anything you can lay your hands on, Norris!'

'Anything, cap'n?' said Norris.

'Yes, Norris! Anything!' yelled Captain Codswallop. 'We've got to hold them off until help arrives!'

Norris looked desperately around the empty decks for something to use as ammunition. 'There isn't much we can use, cap'n, apart from those piles of fish on the *Flying Kipper.*'

'We'll use them, then!' said Captain Codswallop. 'At least we've got plenty of gunpowder to fire them with.'

'Why don't you use some of these brown, lumpy things as well?' said Dick Turnip, as he and his brother appeared from below deck.

'What brown, lumpy things?' said Norris.

'Yes! What brown, lumpy things?' said Captain Codswallop.

'These brown, lumpy things!' said Dick. He held out his hand. Sitting on his palm was a really strange-looking object. It was a pinkish-brown colour and about the size of a goose egg. It was very lumpy and there were warty blemishes all over its surface.

'Uurgh! Put it away this minute!' exclaimed the captain. 'I've never seen anything like it in my life. It's absolutely disgusting! What is it?'

'I've no idea,' said Dick. 'We found lots of them in the chests you've got stored below deck. The ones with Sir Walter Raleigh's coat of arms painted on the lid.'

'Those must be the chests we borrowed from the merchant ships in the Bay of Biscuits,' said Norris. 'I was wondering whose coat of arms that was.'

'You shouldn't have been looking there!' Captain Codswallop roared at the Turnip brothers. 'Those are *our* treasure chests! They're full of *our* gold and silver.

'No, they're not!' said Nick. 'They're full of thousands and thousands of these brown, lumpy things! They're not full of treasure at all.'

'Yes, they are!' roared the captain. 'We know they are. We opened one!'

'We'd better check the rest of them, cap'n,' said Norris. 'Just to be sure. After all, we only opened one of them, didn't we?'

Captain Codswallop, Norris and the Turnip brothers rushed below deck and began opening the rest of the chests. Every single one was full of brown, lumpy things!

'I think we must have struck lucky when we opened the first one, cap'n,' said Norris.

'Sir Walter must have brought these brown things back from his trip to the New World,' said Dick. 'That gold and silver you found in the first chest was probably just what was left over from his spending money.'

Suddenly, there was a series of enormous bangs above deck, followed by the sound of wood splintering and men shouting wildly. The *Grumpy Roger* began to rock violently and a pirate's pale and terrified face appeared at the hatch above them.

'We're under attack again, captain!' he yelled. 'A cannonball has just hit the main mast!'

As Norris attempted to steer the damaged *Grumpy Roger* into the cover of another fog bank, the Turnip brothers and the pirates loaded the cannons with as many fish and brown, lumpy things as they could stuff in. Then they added the gunpowder and stood by with flaming torches at the ready.

Captain Codswallop braced himself on the bridge with his hand raised, waiting for the right moment to give the signal to open fire. He didn't have to wait long. A gust of wind whipped away the curtain of smoke and fog and once more they were face to face with the admiral's flagship and the rest of the Spanish Armada. Smoke and flames instantly leapt from the sides of the Spanish galleons and cannonballs whizzed over the pirates' heads.

'Ready ... steady ... FIRE!' barked the captain.

The *Grumpy*'s eight cannon roared into life and the air was immediately filled with flying fish and bits of the brown, lumpy things. Moments later the Spaniards were splattered with the full force of the pirates' bombardment.

Most of it hit the admiral's boat! It was blasted by a broadside of bream. Slammed by a salvo of shrimp. Walloped by a volley of whitebait. And showered with a storm of bits of brown, lumpy things. Finally ... it was clobbered by a cannonade of cod!

'Yes, you've been CODSWALLOPED! That'll teach you to pick on us pirates!' yelled the captain, and the crew of the *Grumpy Roger* gave a big cheer.

Seconds later, and much to the surprise of the pirates and highwaymen, the Spanish guns all fell silent.

'Surely we can't have beaten them already?' said Dick Turnip.

'They probably don't know what's hit them!' laughed Captain Codswallop. He paused and sniffed the air, then said, 'Hmmm. What is that *delicious* smell?'

'What smell, cap'n?' said Norris, wrinkling his nose. 'The only thing I can smell is smoke and spent gunpowder. Then again, I have had a cold since I fell in the Thames.'

'I can smell it now!' said Dick Turnip, taking a deep breath. 'Delicious, isn't it? I wonder where it's coming from?'

'I can smell it, too,' said Nick, licking his lips. 'It's making me feel really hungry! I love food, I do!'

'Yes, so do I!' said Captain Codswallop, patting his tummy. 'What's your favourite?'

'Well?' said Nick, ' I'm rather partial to my mum's steak and kidney pudding, she does it with—'

'Excuse me, gentlemen!' said Norris. 'It may have escaped your attention, but we just happen to be in the middle of a life-or-death battle. The Spaniards are probably reloading at this very moment!'

'He's right, you know!' said Captain Codswallop. 'We'd better do the same!'

As they crammed the last of the 'ammunition' into the sizzling-hot barrel of a cannon, Norris said, 'That's odd!'

'What's odd?' said Dick.

'The Spanish still haven't started firing,' said Norris. 'I'd have thought they'd be trying to blast us out of the water by now. I wonder what can be keeping them?'

'You're right!' said Dick. 'They're suspiciously quiet, aren't they?'

'There are some noises coming from their boats,' said Nick. 'Listen!'

'Shooting starfish!' cried Captain Codswallop. 'I can hear cutlasses being rattled. And muskets being fired! The Spaniards must be preparing to board us!'

'I don't think they are, cap'n,' said Norris. 'It sounds more like they're rattling knives and forks and pulling corks from bottles.'

'You're right!' said Dick. 'If I didn't know better, I'd say they'd stopped for lunch.'

'Stopped for lunch!?' spluttered the captain. 'But that's impossible! They're in the middle of a battle. Hmmmm! I wish I knew what that delicious smell was.'

Now that the smoke from the gunpowder had drifted away, the tempting smell was even stronger. Dick and Nick were almost swooning with hunger as the mouthwatering aromas floated across the water, and the pirates were licking their lips and saying things like, 'Cor I'm absolutely starving I am!' and 'That's the perfectest pong I've ever set my nostrils on!'

Even Norris got a whiff of it now. 'Cor! It really is yummy, isn't it?' he said, and suddenly had an idea. He picked up Captain Codswallop's telescope and peered towards the admiral's flagship. An astonishing sight met his eye. All over the admiral's ship and the other galleons, the Spaniards were sitting at long tables and tucking into what was obviously a very tasty lunch.

They seemed to have completely forgotten about the battle they'd been fighting only five minutes earlier.

'Well, I never!' Norris gasped. 'You were right, Dick! The Spaniards have stopped for lunch!'

'Here, let me have a look!' said the captain, taking the telescope and putting it to his own eye. 'Well, splice my braces and jiggle my jib!' he exclaimed. 'Whatever it is, they're shovelling it down like there's no tomorrow. I've never heard of anything like this before, especially in the middle of a sea battle! Then again, that admiral was a bit of a strange cove. Two spars short of a mizzen mast, if you ask me!'

'Talking of him!' said Norris. 'There's a boat putting out from his flagship at this very moment! It's flying a white napkin, too. And Admiral Don Alfonso De Torremolinos is on board. He's looking very pleased with himself. What on ocean can he want?'

CHAPTER ELEVEN

Three minutes later, Admiral Don Alfonso De Torremolinos's rowing boat arrived at the *Grumpy Roger*. As his sailors tied a mooring rope to the pirate ship, he grinned up at Captain Codswallop and said, 'Greetings, my good friend, Sir Fancy Drinks. May I be coming aboard, please? I am promising you I will not be giving you any panky-hanky. Cross my harp and hope to fry!'

He waved a white handkerchief at Captain Codswallop and grinned again.

'Well I suppose so,' said Captain Codswallop. 'But you better watch it! We're armed to the teeth. And we're very, very fierce!'

'Sir Fancy,' said Admiral Don Alfonso de Torremolinos, as he climbed aboard the *Grumpy Roger* and grasped Captain Codswallop by the hand. 'My men and me have just beens gobblings the tastiest, nicestest blanket we have ever enjoyed in our whole lives!'

'There you go, Norris,' whispered Captain Codswallop. 'I told you he was as barmy as a barnacle. They've been eating their own blinking bedclothes!'

'Actually I think he means banquet, cap'n,' said Norris.

'Yes, that is it ... banquet!' cried Admiral Torremolinos. 'It was a feast fit for kings! And now we have come for the peas!'

'We 'aven't got any blinkin' peas,' said Captain Codswallop.

'I think he means the peace,' said Norris. 'It looks like he wants to call a truce.'

'Yes, that is it. You are right, little curly-top cabin bunny,' said Admiral Torremolinos, patting Norris on the head. 'We are no more the fightings with you. We is lovings you for the wonderful, tasty banquet gift you have sended to us! And now we is finished for ever the big up-punch. We is now shookings your hand and givings you bigs, bigs kissings!'

And with that the admiral put his arms around Captain Codswallop and gave him a big hug followed by a long, sloppy kiss on both cheeks. The captain went bright red and the

Turnip brothers and the crew of the *Grumpy Roger* started to snigger.

Big tears were now rolling down the admiral's cheeks. He put his hands on the captain's shoulders and said, 'Sir Fancy Drinks, you is givings us the too much kindness and we is lovings you. We have been goings alls over the world and doing the fightings with the Toms, Diegos and Heinrichs. But you is the firsts peoples what is kind enough to be givings us the lunches in the middles of the battle. And what a scrummy up-nosh it is being! Yum, yum, yummy, yum, yum! Talkings about tasty! My mens is lickings their tums and pattings their lips and doings the big burpings! They is much happy. What is you calling the beautifully cooked fishes with the scrummy, hot, golden vegetables slivers what we is puttings in our mouths and then goings to heavens?'

The captain looked totally bewildered and said, 'Err, I haven't the foggiest?'

Quick-thinking Norris coughed, then swiftly said, 'What the captain means is that we've not decided yet, Admiral Torremolinos. It's an exciting new recipe that we've just invented in honour of you and your brave fighting men and, quite naturally, we wanted you to be the first to taste it. We're delighted you enjoyed it!'

'Certainly did!' said the admiral, as he took the captain's hand and shook it firmly. 'So I am now givings you the *adios*. We are goings away now. We are not doings the fightings on you Hinglish no mores. You is our friendships.

'You is too kindness to be the anemones. And wherever we is goings, we will be tellings all the peoples over the world about this great English scrummy up-nosh made of the beautifully cooked fishes with the scrummy, hot, golden vegetables slivers.' Then he cleared his throat and, looking slightly embarrassed, added, 'But before we is goings we is stills a bit peckishes. Could you be sending the seconds? Just a tinsy blastings please?'

•

The crew of the *Grumpy Roger* had just delivered a final blast of lunch to the Spanish fleet and waved them farewell when they heard a *beep, beep* noise.

Captain Codswallop scanned the ocean with his telescope and spotted Ginger Hale in his rowing boat. He was grinning from ear to ear, waving madly and pointing over his shoulder. The entire English Navy was following him. They were coming to the rescue. They needn't have bothered though, the Spanish Armada was just disappearing over the horizon and the pirates were already busily tidying up after the battle.

'We're for it now!' said Dick Turnip, with a worried glance towards the approaching English war fleet. 'The moment that lot arrive, me and Nick are bound to be arrested and taken before the queen!'

'You're right, Dick!' said Nick, looking around in panic. 'And this time, we've nowhere to run!'

'Oh, I wouldn't worry,' said Norris, with a reassuring smile. 'Once Queen Elizabeth finds out that you've helped see off the Spaniards, she'll be only too happy to forget about your little mistake.'

'I'm sure Norris is right, lads,' said Captain Codswallop. 'After all, he's been right about everything else, hasn't he?'

As the last of the Spanish galleons' sails disappeared from sight, Norris picked up one of the brown, lumpy objects and examined it thoughtfully. He had a strange feeling that something very important had just taken place. Something so important that it would still be remembered and talked about in hundreds of years' time. 'Do you realise what's just happened, cap'n?' he said to Captain Codswallop.

'Yes I do, Norris, I do!' said the captain. 'I've just been kissed by the admiral of the Armada. And I'm not too happy about it!'

'No, cap'n, not that!' said Norris. 'This is far more important!'

'What, Norris?' exclaimed Captain Codswallop, looking rather bewildered.

'Two great events in British History have just taken place!' said Norris. 'And it's all thanks to us!'

'Is it?' said Captain Codswallop, raising his eyebrows in amazement.

'Yes, cap'n, it is!' said Norris proudly. 'Do you realise that we have just been responsible for the defeat of the mighty Spanish Armada?'

'Have we?' said Captain Codswallop. 'Wow!'

'But that's not all, cap'n!' continued Norris.

'Isn't it?' said the captain, beginning to look confused again.

'No it's not,' said Norris. 'We have also done something else. While we were bravely doing battle with that terrifying war fleet, we also invented a delicious meal, consisting of cooked fish served with hot, golden fragments of these brown, lumpy things. I have the strange feeling that in years to come this dish will become famous throughout the land. One day, in the not-too-distant future, shops will open in every town and village, just to sell this scrumptious nosh.'

'Cor!' said Captain Codswallop.

'The only thing is,' added Norris. 'I've no idea what the new dish will be called.'

'Er, how about fish 'n' slivers?' said Captain Codswallop.

A WORD FROM THE AUTHOR

I wrote this story because, about 50 years ago, I used to be a pirate … but only on Wednesday afternoons.

When our PE teachers were in a good mood, they'd let us play a great game called 'Pirates'. We'd put out all the big gym apparatus, such as dangly ropes, criss-cross rigging, planks and whatnot so that the whole lot ended up looking like two dirty, great pirate ships and someone would be picked to be the 'pirate'. They had to try and 'dob'★ everyone else as they scrambled up and down the rigging and leapt from boat to boat, yelling and bellowing like batty buccaneers. If you fell into the sea (or 'hall floor', as boring people called it) or got dobbed, you had to join the pirates and it all carried on until only one person was left undobbed and they were the winner.

I also used to be a highwayman, but I didn't have a horse, so I had to rely on boy called Darren Dobbs, who would gallop after local stagecoaches (i.e. the bin men's lorry and the milkman's horse and cart) with me on his back, but only if I fed him sugar lumps and carrots.

The other reason I wrote the story is because of my interest in history and sillyness. You can't always trust history books and people always give their own version of a historical event, usually the one that makes them look really good. It occured to me that Sir Francis Drake may well have defeated the Spanish Armada with a bit of help from someone like Captain Codswallop, but preferred to take all the credit himself. After all it is only history (or *his* story?).

*NB: Important health and safety note: just in case you don't know, 'dob' means to tap someone lightly, not run them through with a cutlass or chuck them out of the crow's nest.

I Am a Tree

KAYE UMANSKY

*"They've cast the school play
and I'm a tree!"*

Tim's an ace actor and usually gets the lead
role in the school play, so he's shocked to
find out that this time he's been cast as a tree.
And, what's worse, the only lines he has to
speak are in rhyming couplets! Can anything
be done to help Tim save face, or does this
mean curtains for his acting career?

Black Cats
Books to pounce on

James and the Alien Experiment

Sally Prue

"The bony hand zoomed right out of the screen and grabbed him."

When James is kidnapped by aliens, he can't believe his luck. They want to transform his feeble human body and James can have whatever superpowers he likes. He chooses super-speed, super-brains and super-strength. But James soon starts to realise he might have got slightly more than he asked for...

Black Cats

Books to pounce on

Spooks Away

SUE PURKISS

*"Those who enter Inverscreech should be wary.
Those walls contain some deep, dark secrets."*

Young ghosts Spooker, Goof and Holly are
off to a remote Scottish castle to make a
video about how to haunt. But the castle
turns out to be less lonely than expected. The
arrival of a bunch of Americans and a series
of spooky goings on give the ghosts rather
more to deal with than they bargained for…

Black Cats
Books to pounce on

Bryony Bell's Star Turn

FRANZESKA G. EWART

*"It's just as well Yours Truly has a breathtakingly
brilliant, scintillatingly surefire gem of an idea
up her sleeve."*

There's never a dull moment in the Bell
household. Fresh from success on Broadway, they
now star in their very own reality TV show. Plus
there's the mystery of Ken Undrum's long lost
love to solve, the Nativity play to rehearse, and
Bryony has special plans to make sure the
coming Christmas will be full of surprises…

Black Cats
Books to pounce on

100% PIG

Tanya Landman

"Oh, Terence. I'm really going to miss you."

Terence the Tamworth boar is proud to
be 100% pig. But his cosy life on the
rare breeds farm is about to change the
day a lorry comes to take him away.
Can Terence escape before it's too late?
And, if he does, how will he cope
with being a pig on the run?

Black Cats
Books to pounce on

Time
AND AGAIN
Rob Childs

"By a click of the clock, You can go in reverse,
Time and Again, For better or worse."

With the discovery of a strange-looking
watch, twins Becky and Chris gain the
power to travel back in time. It's the
opportunity to relive events and put things
right. But trying to change the past doesn't
always work out as the twins intend.
Especially when class troublemaker
Luke is around…

Black Cats
Books to pounce on

Black Cats
Books to pounce on